CAN YOU SMELL BREAKFAST?

written by Edward Jazz
dedicated to Eevee & Tho

illustrated by Gill Guile
dedicated to Anya

Can You Smell Breakfast? copyright © by Kids Books Rule!, 2022.
All rights reserved.

ISBN: 978-1-7373255-2-9 (paperback)
ISBN: 978-1-7373255-3-6 (hardcover)

This book is a work of fiction. Names, characters, places and incidents are either the product of the author's imagination or are used fictitiously, and any resemblance to actual persons, living or dead, business establishments, events or locales is entirely coincidental.

Visit us online at www.kidsbooksrule.com

Ivy loves her bunny, the color pink, rainbows, watching tv (especially shows that she's not allowed to watch), and playing chess.

But, most of all, Ivy loves breakfast.

"Where's Daddy?" Ivy asked.

"He's downstairs cooking. Can you smell breakfast?" asked her mother.

"I smell cupcakes!" said Ivy. "I hope they have tons of pink icing!"

"I smell pancakes," said her mother. "I hope they are not covered in icing."

"I smell a banana split!" said Ivy with a giggle. "I hope Dad doesn't slip on the peel!"

"I smell a fruit smoothie," said her mother, yawning.

"I smell nachos!" said Ivy. "I hope they are hot, then I can be a dragon!"

"I smell toast," said her mother. "I hope it isn't burned."

"I smell pizza!" said Ivy. "I will share it with you and my bunny."

"I smell avocado toast," said her mother. "Does your bunny like that?"

"I smell chili cheese fries! Yum yummy!" said Ivy hopefully, crossing her fingers.

"Hmm, I think I smell oatmeal," said her mother.

"Maybe I smell cookies!" Ivy said. "With chocolate chips and cinnamon swirls!"

"I smell croissants, fluffy and light," said her mother.

"I smell cotton candy, like we had at the fall festival!" said Ivy. "Remember when I got it stuck in my hair?"

"Yeah...Let's forget about that," said her mother. "I smell orange juice."

"I smell spaghetti!" said Ivy. "Dad always makes great spaghetti! I can whirl it and slurp it."

"Not in my bed," said her mother. "I smell fresh strawberries, my favorites."

"Do I smell potato chips?" asked Ivy. "I could eat them all day."

"I smell French toast," said her mother. "Ooh la la! I hope we can visit Paris one day."

"And eat Mille-Feuille as tall as the room!" Ivy laughed and bounced on the bed with her bunny.

meel-foy

"Who wants breakfast?" yelled Dad from the kitchen.

"We do!" said Ivy and her mother as they ran downstairs.

Turning the corner they both gasped in delight!

On the table was EVERYTHING they smelled.

Even the bunny smiled when he saw the amazing breakfast.

www.kidsbooksrule.com

SPECIAL INVITATION

Be the first to receive updates from Kids Books Rule!, including free giveaways, new release announcements, behind-the-scenes goodies, and much more!

Visit the secret link below to join:
www.kidsbooksrule.com/smell

A NOTE FROM THE AUTHOR

Thank you so much for your support. Every time you purchase from an independent author, someone is celebrating on the other end (me)!

If you loved this book, please consider leaving a review so that other readers will take a chance on this 5 Senses Book Series for kids.

www.kidsbooksrule.com/review

Thank you so much!
Edward Jazz

Printed in the USA
CPSIA information can be obtained
at www.ICGtesting.com
LVHW070902031123
762879LV00055B/23